S0-BZI-743

LUCY
THE BABY DEER

Story by Robert E. Maunus

Illustrated by Lon Eric Craven

~ Danvers Massachusetts ~

Copyright © 2008 Robert E. Maunus

All rights reserved. No part of this book may be reproduced in any form or by any electronic means, including information storage and retrieval systems, photocopying and recording, graphic and mechanical, without the permission in writing from the author and publisher, except by a reviewer who may quote brief passages in a review.

ISBN   0-9821073-8-2

          978-0-9821073-8-6

February 2009

This book has been illustrated by Lon Eric Craven. He is represented by WendyLynn & Co., www.wendylynn.com

Book design and layout by IDT Design, robin@robinwrighton.com
Text set in ITC New Baskerville, printed on acid free paper.
Printed by King Printing Company, Inc., www.kingprinting.com

Published and printed in the United States of America

To my daughter Elissa, the real little girl.

~ R.E.M.

About the Author:

Bob has loved dogs his whole life. He spends way too much time running them, playing with them, thinking about them and writing about them. He lives with his family and dog, Bones, in Massachusetts.

To Melody, my beautiful wife,
for your patience and inspiration.

~ L.E.C.

About the Illustrator:

Lon Eric Craven lives in Kansas City, Missouri, with his wife and three children. The youngest daughter and the family dog, Jack, helped bring "Lucy" to life as they acted out the scenes of the little girl and Bones for the artist. Lon Eric has a BFA in illustration from the University of Kansas and a Master's degree in education from the State University of New York at Buffalo. He has illustrated and designed for newspapers, children's books, English language curriculum, story books, quilt books, calendars and a Scholastic magazine. He currently divides his time between illustrating, designing and teaching.

LUCY
THE BABY DEER

Story by Robert E. Maunus

Illustrated by Lon Eric Craven

Dad and I drove with Bones, our puppy, to the canal that runs through the big woods. We got out of the car and Bones ran fast down the path. It was a nice warm day in May. Bones was running this way and that and soon his tongue was hanging out. He was so hot!

We walked far along the path into the cool woods. Dad and I sat down on a fallen tree trunk to have a cold drink of water. Suddenly, little Bones stopped snuffling through the brush and pointed into the deep, dark woods.

Slowly, a little spotted baby deer came out of the woods and sniffed Bones.

Dad was smiling, "What a lovely baby deer! It's called a fawn," he said. "We have to leave now so the mother deer can take care of her baby."

We walked away from the fawn and went back to the car. As we got in, we could see that the baby deer had followed and was standing at the edge of the trees looking at us.

The minute we got home, I ran into the kitchen and told Mom that we had seen a baby deer! She was happy for us and said, "If you're lucky, you might see her again." We had dinner, then I did my homework before going to bed.

The next day after school, I took three books out of the library about deer. I was so excited! I learned that the mother deer sometimes leaves the baby alone for a bit while she gathers food. She comes back soon to take care of her baby. I learned that baby deer can run very soon after they are born and are good at hiding in the woods.

I asked Dad to take us to the woods again and he smiled. He wanted to see the fawn again too.

We walked along the same path through the trees and sure enough, we saw the fawn again! This time she hopped right over to Bones and licked his face. She was twirling her tail, "Swish, swish."

Bones was wagging his tail so hard I thought it would break! Dad spent a lot of time walking all around while Bones and I watched the fawn. Dad seemed to be looking for something. Too soon, it was time to go.

This time the fawn followed us much farther, almost to the car. Dad was not smiling now, and he looked worried as he glanced along the edge of the trees.

As soon as we got home, I told Mom all about seeing the fawn again! She was light brown with little white spots all over her back, a tiny white freckle on her face, and shiny black hooves that almost looked like shoes. Dad looked worried as he told Mom he didn't see the baby's mother anywhere.

Over the next few days, I read more and more about deer and what they do and what they eat. Baby deer are called fawns and are born in May. Fawns stay with the mother for about one year before going off on their own. They eat many different kinds of plants and even tree bark in the winter. A grownup deer can jump eight feet high and as far as thirty feet! I got to know all about deer!

Three days later, Dad said it was time to go to the canal again. Yay! As soon as we got there, Bones jumped out of the car and ran as fast as he could all the way up the path. Right away we heard, "Maaa, Maaaa," from the bushes and out came the fawn!

Just like before, Bones went, "Wag, wag, wag," and the fawn went, "Swish, swish." This time Dad took a long, long time looking in the woods and far up and down the path. He looked very worried.

All too soon, it was time to go. This time the fawn did not follow us, but walked right WITH us, all the way to the car. The fawn stood there looking at us as we got into the car. Dad looked very serious. He stood there a long time.

All of a sudden he picked up the fawn and put her in the back seat with Bones and me. The deer put her head on Bones and fell fast asleep. I was very surprised!

When we got home, Dad carried the deer, who was still fast asleep, into our living room and laid her on the floor by the fireplace. Bones curled up beside her and fell fast asleep too.

Soon Mom came home. She started unloading the groceries when the fawn woke up. As she walked into the kitchen, "Tap, tap, tap," went her tiny hooves on the floor. She twirled her tail, "Swish, swish, swish." Mom looked up in amazement! Dad was smiling!

Mom looked over at Dad and said, "What? How? Who?"

"I looked every day and I couldn't find the fawn's mother. They need help for at least one year. I couldn't leave her alone," Dad said, looking sheepish.

Mom looked very surprised and said, "Are you trying to start a zoo?"

Dad said, "No, we just want to help her until she can be on her own."

We watched as the fawn began to inspect her new home. She walked around and sniffed every corner of the house with Bones following just like her shadow.

After a full inspection, the fawn said, "Maaaaaa, Maaaaaaa!" Mom took my old baby bottle from the kitchen cupboard and poured milk into it. She heated it up on the stove and gave it to me. I fed the baby deer and she loved it! "Swish, swish!" I told Mom, "I'm going to call her Lucy." Mom said, "Every baby needs a nice name."

That night, Lucy curled up with Bones by the fireplace and they slept together like brother and sister.

As the weeks went by, Lucy played with Bones in the huge field behind our house. Bones would chase Lucy and she would jump SO HIGH, clicking her heels together. "Click, click!" Bones would bark, "Roo, Roo!"

Lucy began to drink more and more milk! Our whole kitchen was full of baby bottles. Mom said, "Lucy drinks more milk than you ever did!"

Lucy liked to come with us for walks along the canal. At first Bones could run much faster. But before long, Lucy grew taller and by October she was very big and VERY fast. She had also lost almost all of her spots.

One weekend, Dad and I put a fence up in part of the back yard. This would keep Lucy close to us and protect her from other animals.

Lucy really loved Bones! They would often play tug-of-war with one of Dad's old socks.

Lucy grew fast! She drank less and less milk and began to eat the grass in our fields. Dad was happy; he did not use his mower once!

One day Lucy ate all the corn in our garden. Another time, Mom came home to find all the flowers missing from the pots on the porch. The hedge in front of the house was almost bare because Lucy liked those leaves the best!

When winter came and snow covered all the grass, Dad brought hay for Lucy to eat. Mom said, "At least the hay is outside, not like all the baby bottles!"

Lucy still liked to sleep inside with Bones on cold winter nights. She would rumple the rug by the fire with her hooves and circle around three times before lying down. She began to wear out the rug from pawing it!

That winter Lucy grew very tall and could steal food from the kitchen table.

One day I came home from school to find Bones and Lucy standing on the sofa watching for me out the window. Mom said, "She does that a lot lately."

When Spring came, we took Lucy with us to the woods every other day. Each day she would not follow as closely. One day Lucy looked at us, her tail going, "Swish, swish," then ran off into the woods. She looked over her shoulder like she wanted us to follow. We waited a long, long time but Lucy did not come back. Dad was crying. I never saw Dad cry before.

I was happy. My baby Lucy was all grown up now. It's May again and a whole year has passed.

We didn't see Lucy all summer, but we did see lots of deer tracks in the area near the canal.

That fall was the best ever. The trees were covered with leaves of all colors. Bones had grown into a big, strong dog too! We loved playing in the leaves together. Every time we went for a walk along the canal, Bones and I would search high and low, but never saw Lucy or any other deer.

The winter was cold and snowy right from the start. I would often sit by the fire and look at the worn out spot on the rug. I missed Lucy.

Dad came home one day and told me to get my coat. Bones and I got in the car, which was loaded up with hay bales. Dad drove us to the canal where we dragged four bales of hay up the path into the woods. Dad said, "I'm afraid Lucy might be hungry since the snow is so deep." We wanted her to have enough to eat.

Two days later we went back and there were FRESH deer tracks all over the snow near the hay. Half of the hay had been eaten! I was very excited.

Every Saturday Dad and I pulled four bales of hay into the woods by the canal. Hay is very heavy! We dragged it on the ice when we could. People said it was the hardest winter in 50 years.

Finally the snow began to melt away and Spring was in the air. The birds were singing again and the paths were muddy. We stopped bringing the hay. Dad said there was now lots of food for all the animals. We didn't see Lucy, but we did see deer tracks in the mud.

One fine day in May we went back to the canal for a walk. Bones ran right to the path and wagged his tail. He barked once, "Roo." Out of the woods stepped Lucy, with her own little baby! The new baby had the same tiny freckle on her face, just like Lucy.

Lucy twirled her tail, "Swish, swish." The baby wagged her tail, "Swish, swish." Bones stood there wagging from head to tail with excitement.

Dad was crying again, but this time he was smiling too.

All too soon, Lucy and her fawn walked quietly back into the woods. We drove home in silence.

I did not sleep that night. I thought about finding things and letting them go. I thought about loving someone and still letting them go. I thought of how lucky I was to have Lucy, even for a little while.

When the sun started coming up, I thought of Lucy making her new life with her baby and I smiled as I drifted off to sleep.

TO THE READER: Never approach ANY wild animal, big or small. They may feel threatened, defend themselves and be very dangerous!

There really is a Bones